W9-BPR-731

Teletubbies™

Here Come the Teletubbies

Illustrations by John Youssi.

Text adapted from the original scripts
by Andrew Davenport.

SCHOLASTIC INC.

New York   Toronto   London   Auckland   Sydney

No part of this publication may be reproduced in whole or in part,
or stored in a retrieval system, or transmitted in any form or by any means,
electronic, mechanical, photocopying, recording, or otherwise, without written
permission of the publisher. For information regarding permission, write to
Scholastic Inc., Attention: Permissions Department, 555 Broadway, New York, NY 10012.

ISBN 0-590-38623-9

Teletubbies character and logo, copyright and TM 1998 Ragdoll Productions (UK) Ltd.
Licensed by The itsy bitsy Entertainment Company. All rights reserved.
Published by Scholastic Inc.
SCHOLASTIC and associated logos are trademarks
and/or registered trademarks of Scholastic Inc.

12 11 10 9 8 7 6 5 4 3 2 1

8 9/9 0 1 2 3/0

Printed in the U.S.A.

First Scholastic printing, October 1998

Over the hill and far away,
Teletubbies come to play.

The Teletubbies love their favorite things.
Tinky Winky loves his bag. Dipsy loves his hat.

Laa-Laa loves her ball.
Po loves her scooter.

He hadn't gone very far,
when he saw Dipsy's hat.

So Tinky Winky put the hat into his bag.

Hat in bag!

He hadn't gone very far,
when he saw Dipsy's hat.

So Tinky Winky put the hat into his bag.

Hat in bag!

Then Tinky Winky saw Laa-Laa's ball.

Look!
Laa-Laa's ball!

So Tinky Winky put the ball into his bag.

Ball in bag!

Then Tinky Winky saw Po's scooter.

Look! Scooter!

So Tinky Winky put the scooter into his bag.

Scooter in bag!

Dipsy, Laa-Laa, and Po were looking
everywhere for their favorite things.

Where hat?

Where ball?

Where
scooter?

Dipsy looked at the top of the hill.
No hat.

No hat!

Dipsy looked at the bottom of the hill.
No hat.

Laa-Laa looked
behind the tree.
No ball.

No ball!

Laa-Laa looked
in front of the tree.
No ball.

No ball!

Po looked next to the flowers.
No scooter.

No scooter!

Po looked between the flowers.
No scooter.

No scooter!

Where was Dipsy's hat?
Where was Laa-Laa's ball?
Where was Po's scooter?

Where hat?

Just then, Tinky Winky
came by, carrying his bag.
It was very heavy.

Dipsy, Laa-Laa, and Po ran over
to help Tinky Winky.

Po didn't know why Tinky Winky's
bag was so heavy.
So she looked inside the bag.

Ooooh!

And she pulled out her scooter!

Scooter!

Laa-Laa looked inside the bag.
And she pulled out her ball!

Ball!

Dipsy looked inside the bag.
And he pulled out his hat!

Hat!

Dipsy, Laa-Laa, and Po thanked Tinky Winky
for bringing them their favorite things.

Ooooh!
Thank you, Tinky Winky.

The Teletubbies love each other very much!

Big Hug!

Bye-bye, Tinky Winky.
Bye-bye, Dipsy.
Bye-bye, Laa-Laa.
Bye-bye, Po.

Bye-bye!

Bye-bye!